This book belongs to

....

LADYBIRD BOOKS

UK | USA | Canada | Ireland | Australia | India | New Zealand | South Africa

Ladybird Books is part of the Penguin Random House group of companies
whose addresses can be found at global.penguinrandomhouse.com.

www.penguin.co.uk   www.puffin.co.uk   www.ladybird.co.uk

Penguin
Random House
UK

First published 2023
001

Licensed by

Printed in China

The authorized representative in the EEA is Penguin Random House Ireland,
Morrison Chambers, 32 Nassau Street, Dublin D02 YH68

A CIP catalogue record for this book is available from the British Library

ISBN: 978-0-241-60716-9

All correspondence to:
Ladybird Books, Penguin Random House Children's
One Embassy Gardens, 8 Viaduct Gardens, London SW11 7BW

George's Digger

One sunny morning, Mummy Pig took Peppa and
George to the shops.
"Now, where shall we pop in first . . . ?" asked Mummy Pig.
"TOY SALE!" shouted Mr Fox. "Discount dolls!
Bargain blocks! Cut-price cuddlies!"

Est. 2010

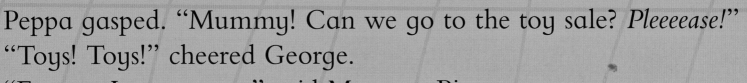

Peppa gasped. "Mummy! Can we go to the toy sale? *Pleeeease!*"

"Toys! Toys!" cheered George.

"Err . . . I suppose so," said Mummy Pig.

It was very busy inside Mr Fox's shop, but Peppa and George had lots of fun looking around.

"You can pick ONE thing each," said Mummy Pig, smiling, "so choose carefully!"

"Thank you, Mummy!" cried Peppa, hurrying off to find a toy.

But George had already spotted something special.
"Dig-ga!" he whispered, picking up a shiny toy digger.
"Excellent choice, George!" said Mr Fox. "That'll be one pound,
please, Mummy Pig!"

After the shopping trip, Mummy Pig took Peppa and
George to Granny and Grandpa Pig's house for the afternoon.
"Hello, little ones," said Grandpa Pig. "Did you have a
nice morning?"

"Yes!" cheered Peppa. "We went to the shops, and I got this! It's a croquet set."

"Dig-ga!" said George, holding up his digger.

"Oh my!" said Granny Pig. "What excellent toys!"

While Peppa and Granny Pig played croquet, Grandpa Pig let George use the digger on his vegetable patch.

"First, dig a little hole in the dirt," said Grandpa Pig.
"Then, pop in a seed!"
"Dig! Dig!" said George, using his digger to make a hole.
"That's perfect, George!" said Grandpa Pig. "Thanks to
your little digger, we'll get these seeds planted in no time!"

When Daddy Pig arrived later to pick up Peppa and George,
a very muddy surprise was waiting for him.

"George and his digger have been helping me in the garden,"
explained Grandpa Pig.
"I see . . ." said Daddy Pig, laughing. "Well, it's a good job
it's bath night!"

At home, George took his digger into the bath and used it to scoop up all the bubbles . . .

Then, at bedtime, he used it to tuck Mr Dinosaur into bed, too! "Night-night, dig-ga," George mumbled as he drifted off to sleep.

The next morning, Daddy Pig had a surprise for Peppa and George.
"I've been designing a new miniature golf course," he said. "It's nearly ready, so I thought we'd go and see it."
But George wanted to stay at home and play with his digger.

Daddy Pig smiled. "You can bring your little digger with you, George. And there'll be a real digger at the construction site, too!"

"Dig-ga!" George cheered, hurrying off to get ready.

The construction site was very busy. Mr Bull and his crew were putting the finishing touches in place.
"DOWN! LEFT! RIGHT! NO – OTHER RIGHT!" bellowed Mr Bull as the crane operator set a little windmill on the course.

"Hello, Mr Bull!" said Daddy Pig. "I've brought Peppa and George for a tour."
"Wonderful," said Mr Bull. "We're nearly done, so I'll show you around myself!"

First, Mr Bull showed them the wrecking ball. "We use this to –"
"*SMASH!*" shouted Peppa and George.
"Exactly!" said Mr Bull. "Knocking things down is fun!"

Next, they visited the cement mixer.
"Cement takes a little while to dry,"
Mr Bull warned. "But it makes
lovely smooth paths!"

Then, he showed them the dump truck. "We use this for moving sand and gravel," he said.

But George wasn't listening.
He had spotted something much more exciting . . .

"DIG-GA!" George cheered, pointing. "It looks just like yours, George!" said Peppa.

"My digger is great for digging big holes," said Mr Bull. "Would you like to give it a try?"

Mr Bull drove the digger, but he let Peppa
and George press some very important buttons.
"DIG! DIG!" George cried as he helped
Mr Bull dig a **humongous** hole.
"We'll fill this with sand," said Mr Bull.
"It'll make a great bunker!"

By the time Peppa and George's tour was complete, a crowd had
gathered for the course's grand opening.
Peppa gasped. "There are so many visitors!"
"It's a good job we finished everything on time!" Mr Bull chuckled.

nip!

Daddy Pig was in charge of cutting the ribbon. He grabbed
a pair of scissors and cleared his throat. "Right," he said,
"I declare this miniature golf course open!"
"Hooray!" everyone cheered.

While the visitors started their games, Mr Bull took Peppa, George and Daddy Pig to his tent for refreshments.
"Would you like some tea?" asked Mr Bull. "Or perhaps some cake?"

Mr Bull had just finished slicing a delicious chocolate cake for everyone when Mr Rhino appeared.

"**Mr Bull! Daddy Pig!**" panted Mr Rhino.

"There's a problem with the course . . ."

Oh dear! Mr Rhino was right.
The construction crew had done an
amazing job on Daddy Pig's design,
but they had forgotten something
very important . . .
"There aren't any holes for the balls,"
cried Peppa.

"Ah," said Mr Bull, scratching his head.
"My digger only digs very big holes. I can't
fix it with that."

Luckily, George had an idea . . .

"Dig-ga!" George cheered suddenly,
waving his little digger in the air.
"Ooh!" said Peppa. "Clever George!"

She whispered George's plan to Daddy Pig and Mr Bull,
and they all squeezed into a nearby golf cart.

Daddy Pig drove them around the course, and George used his little digger to dig perfect little holes in all the right places!

Dig! Dig!

Mr Bull inspected George's work. "My digger is great for digging big holes," he said. "But George's digger is perfect for digging little holes!"

"I declare this miniature golf course
open . . . again!" Daddy Pig told the crowd.
"Hooray!" everyone cheered.
Soon, everyone was having lots of fun
hitting their balls over dinosaurs, through
fairy-tale castles . . . and into George's
freshly dug holes!

Peppa and George had a great time playing
miniature golf together.
"Thank you for saving the day, George!" said
Mr Bull. "Your little digger is fantastic."
"Dig-ga!" cried George happily.

Hee!
Hee!

Ho!
Ho!

George loves his digger.
Everyone loves George's digger!